Published 2004 by Grange Books
an imprint of Grange Books PLC.
The Grange
Kings North Industrial Estate
Hoo nr. Rochester
Kent, UK
ME3 9ND
www.grangebooks.co.uk

All enquiries please email info@grangebooks.co.uk

Copyright ©2004 Taj Books Ltd

All notations of errors or omissions (author inquiries, permissions) concerning the content of this
book should be addressed to:
TAJ Books 27, Ferndown Gardens, Cobham, Surrey, UK, KT11 2BH, info@tajbooks.com.

ISBN 1-84013-704-5

Printed in China.

1 2 3 4 5 08 07 06 05 04

Three Little Pigs

Allison

Grange
BOOKS

Contents

THE LITTLE RED ENGINE

James was a fine red engine. He had two small wheels in front and six driving wheels behind. And, he was able to pull railway coaches and tracks. The coaches aren't easy to manage. They don't like being bumped, and tracks are silly and noisy. They need to be bumped and taught to behave.

This morning James had to take some passenger coaches to another town. And, when the train controller blew his whistle, James started off with a great rush.

"Don't go so fast, don't go so fast, don't go so fast,"the coaches grumbled, but James rushed on. He did not even want to stop at the first station.

So the first two coaches were away beyond the platform before James stopped, and the driver made him back a little to let the passengers get off on the platform. Then away they started again, James pushing along as fast as he could, his coaches grumbling and clattering behind him until they came to a hill. James puffed, "it's ever so steep, it's ever so steep, it's steep but I'll do it, it's steep but I'll do it." And up the long hill James pulled and pulled the coaches. James called to the coaches, "come along coaches, come along coaches."

"All in good time, all in good time,"grumbled the coaches.

"Come along coaches, come along coaches, come along coaches,"said James.

"You're going too fast, you're going too fast, we're going to stop, we're going to stop, we're going to stop."

James had to stop and the driver got down from the engine and looked to see what was the matter. James was cross with the coaches and he let off steam. And the passengers were cross with the driver, and the coaches were cross with James.

The driver found a leak in the brake pipes and when he had mended it, he got back on to the engine and said, "come on James we'll get these coaches going again." James started off quite gently, and didn't go too fast for the coaches this time, and he glided quietly and carefully into the station. The passengers all got off and James took the coaches on to a siding and left them there. And he thought, "I'm glad to be rid of those grumbling things, always want their own way." The driver called, "come along James there's more work to be done. We've twenty trucks to move along the tracks. Here they are, ready."

"Oh, oh, oh said the trucks," as James backed down on them and the driver coupled them to the red engine.

"Go away, go away little red engine."

"Come along, come along, I've got you, I've got you, I've got you."

"We won't, we won't, we won't," screamed the trucks.

But, James pulled hard and the trucks pulled back as hard as they could. "I can, I will, I can, I will," said James, and slowly but surely, he made those trucks move. Then at last they came to a hill ahead of them.

"Look out for trouble James," said the driver. "Those trucks don't like hills. We'll go fast and get those grumbling trucks up that slope before they know it."

"I'll try to do it, I'll try to do it," puffed James, But, it was hard work and the top of the hill seemed a long way off.

"I think I can do it, I think I can do" puffed James.

"You won't you know, you won't you know, you won't you know," screamed the trucks.

"I've nearly done it, I've nearly done it, I've nearly done it," panted James.

"You can't you know, you can't you know, you can't you know." I've done it you know, I've done it you know, I've done it you know, hoorah!"

But, just then, the driver shut off steam and said, "James, we've lost ten trucks, a coupling must have snapped. Look, the last ten trucks are running back down the hill, come on James."

Carefully the driver backed James down the hill until they reached the runaway trucks. He managed to couple the ten trucks back on to the others. James started up that hill again. As James struggled up the hill he thought,

"how silly these trucks are, I'll do it this time, I'll do it this time." The trucks didn't say anything. They thought they'd better behave. They didn't want to be left behind again.

"We're coming to the top, we're coming to the top, we've got to the top, we've got to the top, we've got to the top, hoorah!"

James puffed at the top but, quietly and quickly he glided down, down the slope keeping those trucks under good control until he glided into the station and round onto the siding to leave the trucks for the night.

The driver said, "you're a good little red engine James, I'd never have managed those trucks without you. See you in the morning. Oh, I think we've got an express to take down South tomorrow. Goodnight James."

"An express, oh a real express to pull tomorrow. Oh, that is an important job to look forward to, a very important job for a little red engine." And with a tired, but happy sigh, James settled down in his shed for the night.

ROBIN HOOD

Robin Hood was a proud outlaw who lived in Sherwood Forest, near Nottingham, England. With Robin Hood lived his friends, Little John, Max the miller's son, Will Stutely, Tom the tinker and many other merry men. In the town of Nottingham the sheriff was thinking up plans to capture Robin Hood.

"If I can only capture that outlaw the King will reward me handsomely. Capture Robin Hood, how can I? I have it, he's the finest archer in the whole country. I'll announce a great shooting match for all the archers within miles around, and the prize will be a beautiful golden arrow. Robin Hood could never resist a contest like that. Send the criers around the whole shire to announce the contest at Nottingham fair."

"Oyez, oyez, ye are all summoned to the fair at Nottingham there to shoot for the golden arrow, oyez, oyez."

When Robin Hood heard about the bow and arrow contest he was eager to join in, inspite of the risk of being captured by the Sheriff. He gathered his merry men together and unfolded his plan.

"Now gather round my merry men. We'll go to this fair. I know the sheriff will be waiting for a risk from me, and all of you. So you Little John will take off your Lincoln green clothes and dress as a beggar. You Will Stutely will dress as a village peasant, and Max the miller's son will dress, well he'll put on the clothes of a holy friar, and Tom, gather some pots and pans and go as a tinker."

"Ho, ho, ho very good."

"And each one of you hide your bow and some arrows, a broad sword or a cudgel, in case of need. The sheriff will be expecting the merry men of Sherwood in their clothes of Lincoln green, and if he discovers us beneath our guise, we may have to fight for our lives against his soldiers. Now, I shall

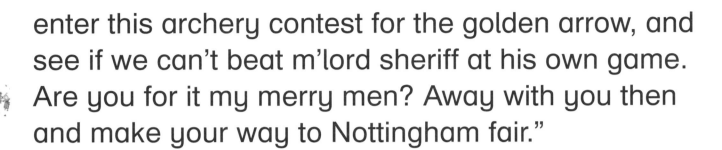

enter this archery contest for the golden arrow, and see if we can't beat m'lord sheriff at his own game. Are you for it my merry men? Away with you then and make your way to Nottingham fair."

"Oyez, oyez, make way for the Sheriff of Nottingham, oyez, oyez. The Sheriff of Nottingham, richly dressed in purple velvet trimmed with fur, a beautiful sea-green silk jacket and with a great golden chain of his office hung about his neck, followed by a hundred friends, soldiers and servants took his seat at the field where the archers stood waiting. At his signal the competing archers lined up facing the targets.

"Let each man shoot one arrow. The ten best of these will then shoot two arrows. From these ten archers the three finalists will compete for the prize of the golden arrow."

While the arrows were being fitted to the bows, the Sheriff carefully searched the face of each archer, looking for the outlaw Robin Hood. There were no men present in the Lincoln green, and he laughed and said that Robin Hood and his men were too cowardly to come out of the forest. Certainly, there were two or three men he had not seen before, that tall man in blue for instance, and the ragged stranger in scarlet with a patch over one eye. Then the crowd at the fair became very silent as they waited for the three finalists to make their winning shots. First Gilbert of the Redcap shot. That was very close to the target centre. Then Adam of the Dell brought his arrowup, aimed and to the delight of the crowd, was even closer to the target. Surely no one could get closer than that. The stranger with the patch over one eye stepped up, took aim and made the perfect shot. The large crowd was quite silent for a moment with amazement and admiration.

"Oyez, oyez, the tattered stranger has won." What is your name my man and where do you come from?"

"Your men do call be Jock of Tivietdale."

"I present you with this golden arrow as champion archer of Nottingham County. If you will join my service, I will give you a new scarlet coat and pay you a wage. Then Robin Hood, the cowardly outlaw, would never again dare show his face in these parts. He dared not come today, that is sure!"

"Nay I will not, no man of merry England shall be my master." Then Robin Hood turned on his heel and strode away. And his merry men dressed as beggars, tinkers and peasants, returned to the forest and prepared a great meal, laughing over the trick they had played on the Sheriff, and admiring the beautiful gold arrow.

"Little John, go you with this note I've written, and when you get near the place where the Sheriff was standing tonight, place this message on the tip of one of your arrows and see that it lands fair in front of the Sheriff."

"It'll please me madly to do this Robin."

That night, the Sheriff was dining with his friends. "Eat up my friends, I thought that outlaw Robin Hood would be at the contest today, he didn't dare. The card let that stupid fellow in rags with the patch over his eye bear away the prize." Just then, an arrow fell among the dishes in front of the Sheriff. He picked up the paper on the arrow tip and read, "now heaven bless the Sheriff this day, say all in green Sherwood, for you did give the prize away to merry Robin Hood."

"Zouns, that ragged one-eyed archer was Robin Hood, I'll be revenged. Call all my archers and my men at arms, we'll go find this rogue in Sherwood. Robin Hood has won this round but the Sheriff of Nottingham will win the next. Where are my archers, my men at arms? Now let Robin Hood beware."

JACK AND THE BEANSTALK

Jack and his mother were very poor indeed. And at last the day came when they had to sell the one cow they had left in order to buy bread. So Jack was sent to market to sell the cow and try to get a good price for it.

Jack was often lazy and thoughtless, and didn't like the long walk driving the cow to market.

On the way he met a butcher who looked at the cow, and offered Jack a handful of strange-looking beans – purple, black and red, in exchange for the cow. He said that the beans were worth a fortune.

When Jack arrived home with a handful of beans and no money or food, his mother was very angry and threw the beans out into the garden.

Both Jack and his mother had to go hungry and sad to bed.

Next morning, when Jack awoke and went outside, he was amazed to find that the beans had taken

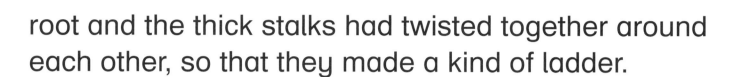

root and the thick stalks had twisted together around each other, so that they made a kind of ladder.

Jack looked up and up and up, but the top of the plant was hidden high behind the clouds.

"I wonder where it ends, I'll climb up and see."

So, Jack climbed up and up and up and up, until right above the clouds he came to the doorway of a great castle. And there stood a tall, tall giantess.

"What do you want and where do you come from? Don't you know my husband is a giant, and he eats little boys?"

"Oh please, I'm so hungry, could I have something to eat?"

"Are you that lazy son of the widow in the cottage way down below?

I suppose you came here to steal back the harp that talks, and the hen that the lays the golden eggs?"

"The harp that talks?"

"Yes, my husband took them from your father years and years ago, just before he died. He took some money too. He won't let you have them back you know. Remember he's a giant, and you're only a boy. But, you're strong and I need someone to work for me. Come in, I'll give you breakfast."

"Yes, I'm very, very hungry."

"But, when my husband the giant comes in, you must hide quickly, get into the great oven. Quickly here he comes, into the oven, he'll never look there."

The ground began to shake and in came the biggest giant you could ever see.

"Wife, I smell meat, Fe-Fi-Fo-Fum I smell the blood of an Englishman. Be he alive or be he dead, I'll grind his bones to make my bread."

"Nonsense husband, you can smell the sheep I killed

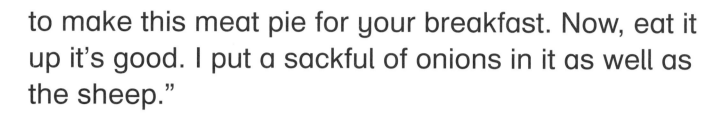

to make this meat pie for your breakfast. Now, eat it up it's good. I put a sackful of onions in it as well as the sheep."

When he had eaten, the giant brought out his money bags and counted his gold before he fell asleep and snored. Jack crept out of the oven, seized the two bags of money and ran to the top of the beanstalk.

He climbed down as fast as he could to his own garden. His mother was overjoyed to see him and delighted to get the money back.

Not long afterwards Jack decided to climb the beanstalk again, and see if he could find the hen that laid the golden eggs, which the giant had stolen from his father.

But, in case the giantess knew him, Jack dyed his hair brown and stained his face brown.

But the giantess still remembered the other boy who had come to the castle, and did not want to have anything to do with this boy. Just then, the house began to shake.

"My husband is coming, he'll eat you. You'd better hide in the cupboard. You can help me with the sweeping later on."

"Wife, I smell fresh meat. Fe-Fe-Fo-Fum I smell the blood of an Englishman. Be he alive or be he head, I'll grind his bones to make my bread."

"There's nobody here, eat your supper."

After supper, the giant called for his wife to bring his magic hen, a beautiful hen with crimson and gold feathers.

"Lay me a golden egg. That's fine, now I shall sleep."

As soon as the giant was asleep Jack picked up his father's magic hen, and climbed quickly down the beanstalk and home to his delighted mother.

Now they could have a golden egg every day and

never be hungry again.

"Mother, I must climb that beanstalk once more and get my father's harp that talks."

"Take care Jack my son, that giant is dangerous. Come, we will dye your hair red this time so they will not recognise you."

Jack knew his way about now and crept into the castle, and hid in a big washing copper under a sheet. "Wife, I smell fresh meat."

"Oh no, I would never let anyone else in here ever again."

"Fe-fi-fo-fum I smell the blood of an Englishman. Be he alive or be he dead, I'll grind his bones to make my bread."

But this time, the giant went searching in every room and cupboard in the castle. He even glanced into the washing copper but saw only the sheet there.

Then, tired out, he ate a huge supper and called for his talking harp to play beautiful music for him. Then he fell fast asleep.

Jack crept out, seized the harp and ran to the door. But the talking harp called out, "master, master."

Gradually the snoring giant wakened up, looked around, opened the door just in time to see Jack climbing down the beanstalk and followed as fast as he was able to.

But Jack reached the ground first. He ran to the shed for a big axe and chopped that beanstalk right through. Down fell that giant from high up on the beanstalk and made a deep, deep hole in the ground. And that was the end of the wicked giant.

Jack and his mother lived happily together and were never hungry again.

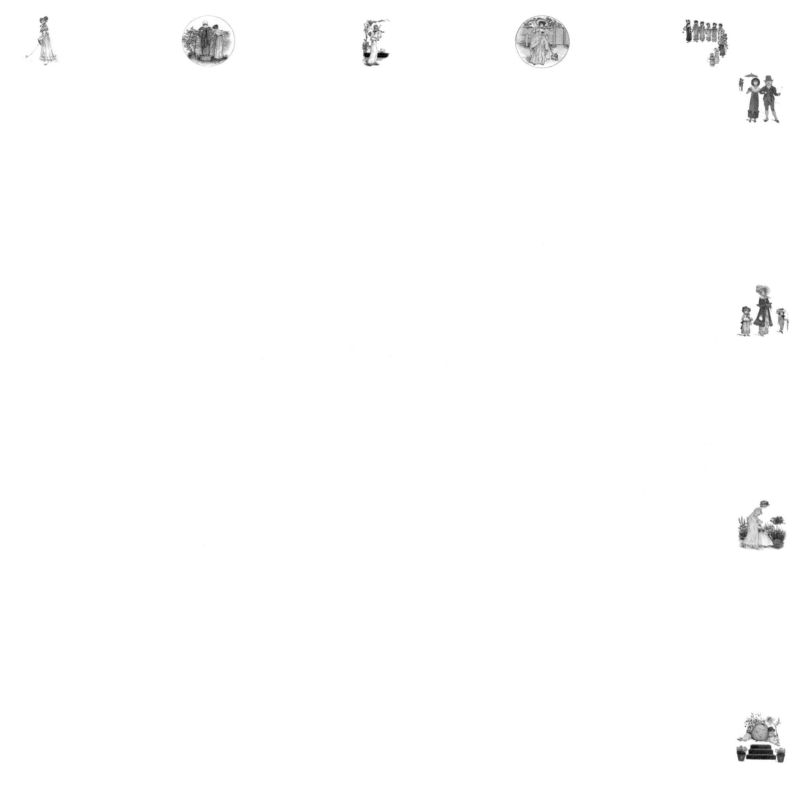

PINOCCHIO

Gepetto the wood carver was just finishing carving a big puppet from a long good, specially good wood.

While he was carving the nose it kept growing longer and longer, even when he carved off the tip. Then he put some hair on the wooden head, and as he painted the eyes blue it seemed to him that the eyes blinked and winked at him.

"That's very funny, I thought my puppet winked. Well, well, nowwhat shall I call him, Pinto, Peppe, no Pinocchio that's it, Pinocchio."

"That's a good name, I like it, Pinocchio."

"Good gracious me, was that you who spoke my puppet?"

"It was and it is, I'm Pinocchio."

"Well, you are a special puppet. I'll tell you what, I'll teach you to walk without strings."

"I feel a bit stiff and new, you know but with practice, well come on let's begin."

So, Gepetto taught Pinocchio to walk. And then he told Pinocchio that it would be good to go to school.

But, he had no money to buy him a spelling book. So while Pinocchio was practising, Gepetto went out, sold his only jacket, and brought back a spelling book.

"Here's your spelling book for school Pinocchio. Now off you go straight down the road to the end, turn left and there you are. Work hard."

"All right. Why are you shivering and where's your jacket. I believe you sold it to buy a spelling book."

Oh, off you go now, and if you work well, you may some day become a real boy instead of a puppet. Goodbye."

"Goodbye."

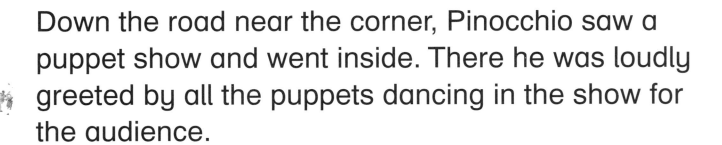

Down the road near the corner, Pinocchio saw a puppet show and went inside. There he was loudly greeted by all the puppets dancing in the show for the audience.

They were amazed that Pinocchio didn't need strings tied to his head and arms and legs to help him to move. And Pinocchio was very pleased with himself, and set to work to show the other puppets how to walk without using the strings.

Their master, Mr. Fireater, was delighted with his clever puppets. And when he found out that Pinocchio had been carved by his old friend Gepetto, and that now he was a very poor man, he gave the puppet some gold coins to take home.

Fireater told Pinocchio to hurry away to school or he would grow to be a donkey, not a boy.

Pinocchio waved goodbye to all the puppets and started off for school, jingling his gold coins. At the corner he was stopped by a fox and a cat who had heard the jingling coins. They asked Pinocchio all kinds of questions as they were determined to get those gold coins for themselves.

"Oh, Pinocchio, are you taking that money home to your father? Would you like to double it? Oh, we can show you how, can't we cat?"

"Oh yes, oh yes, but how?"

"Come with us to the field of the miracles and there we'll bury it. We'll water it with some magic water and tomorrow morning you will dig it up, twice as much gold coins. That's true, isn't it cat?"

So away they went to a field and buried the coins.

Next morning Pinocchio dug and dug but there were no coins at all, and fox and cat were just nowhere to be seen.

They had dug up the coins and run away with them

hours before. Pinocchio sat down in the field of miracles and wept, but that didn't bring back the money or the wicked thieves, fox and cat.

Then just as he was trudging out of the field, he heard a voice. He looked up and saw a large bird hovering around him.

"Why are you weeping puppet, and who are you?"

"I've lost my money. I haven't been to school, and I don't know where my kind father is."

"Is your name Pinocchio?"

"Yes, it is, for why?"

"I was looking for you. I have a message. You had better go and rescue your father, Gepetto. He went looking for you and then he took a boat and rowed towards a small island to search. But a great storm came up, and we don't know whether Gepetto is drowned or swallowed up by a huge fish he saw swimming nearby."

"Oh, oh, I'd do anything to help him. How can I get there? I could float on the water, I'm made of good wood."

"Better get on my back. You won't be too heavy for a while and keep a sharp look-out for a boat near a huge fish."

Pinocchio got astride the bird's back and they searched and searched for days and days with no luck at all. Then as the bird was very tired, Pinocchio decided to swim and float around near an island for a while by himself. He had had a lot of time to think about how kind Gepetto and others had been to him, and how thoughtless he had been. And he promised himself that he would work for Gepetto and go to school. And maybe one day he might be good enough to become a real boy.

While he was thinking sadly about Gepetto he hadn't

noticed that a huge old fish was right beside him. And in a twinkling the fish opened it's great mouth and swallowed Pinocchio. Down he went into a dark, rather damp stomach.

"Oh dear, oh dear, what a dreadful thing to let happen! I must get out and find Gepetto. Was that a noise? It sounded like a voice."

"Hello, is someone here? Hello."

"Well it sounds like, it sounds like Gepetto. Hello, here I am, over here. Oh dear, dear Gepetto. Now don't let us waste any time but get out the next time his huge mouth is opened."

"No Pinocchio, you go. You see, I can't swim."

"Oh, I can float. I'm made of wood and I can hold you up. Besides we're near an island, come on."

Pinocchio was a good swimmer too. And as the old dogfish slept with his mouth open, they soon escaped and floated and swam until they reached the shore. After resting and drying their clothes, Pinocchio went off to find some milk for poor Gepetto. At last he came to a shed where a farmer was milking cows.

But the man made Pinocchio pump water for the farm in payment for the milk. And for months Pinocchio worked hard for food for them both. And after a time, he saved enough to buy new clean jackets and shoes. And then they said goodbye to their friend the farmer, and made their way home to Gepetto's cottage.

With the money he had earned Pinocchio was able to go to school. And Gepetto bought more wood and made some beautiful carvings which he sold in the market. Pinocchio learned so much at school and helped so much at home, that he became a real boy and not a wooden-headed puppet any longer.

LITTLE RED RIDING HOOD

Near a forest there once lived a girl with her father and mother. Her father went into the forest everyday to cut wood to sell. On the other side of the forest lived the little girl's grandmother. She had made her a birthday present of a beautiful little red cloak and a hood. And after that everyone called her 'Little Red Riding Hood.' One day Little Red Riding Hood's mother called her.

"My dear, Granny has not been well, so I want you to go and take this basket of eggs and cream with a little pot of butter and a few cakes. Keep on the path straight to Granny's cottage. Don't talk to anyone on the path and come straight home."

So Little Red Riding Hood put on her cloak and walked through the forest. But on the way she saw some pretty flowers on the side path, and she wandered off to pick some. And there she met a great hungry wolf. The wolf could have eaten her then and there, but he could hear some woodcutters working nearby. So he spoke to Little Red Riding Hood very politely.

"Where are you going my dear?"

Now Little Red Riding Hood forgot that her mother had told her not to talk to anyone she didn't know, especially a wolf. And she replied, "I'm going to my Grandmother's to take her some cakes and eggs and cream, and a little pot of butter."

"Where does she live little girl?"

"In Green Cottage at the edge of the forest."

"What do you do when you get to the cottage?"

"Oh, I knock of course, and Granny says, who is there?"

"What do you do next?"

"I say it's Little Red Riding Hood Granny, and I have brought you some cakes and eggs and cream, and a little pot of butter."

"And what does Granny say?"

"She calls, lift up the latch and come in."

"Well, goodbye Little Red Riding Hood."

The wolf ran off as fast as he could to Grandmother's cottage. But Little Red Riding Hood did not do as her mother told her. She picked flowers, chased butterflies and watched birds flying in the trees, and walked very slowly through the forest. But the wolf soon arrived at the cottage door and knocked. "Who is there?"

"Oh, it's Red Riding Hood. I've brought you some cakes and eggs and cream."

"Oh, lift up the latch and come in."

The wolf opened the door, sprang on the bed and was just about to gobble up Red Riding Hood's Grandmother when he heard someone coming. So he quickly bound a scarf around her mouth, and bundled Granny into a big cupboard and locked it. Then he put her spectacles on his long nose, and pulled her nightcap well over his eyes. Quickly he jumped into her bed, pulling the sheet right up to his chin. Soon there came a knock on the door.

"Who is there?"

"It's Red Riding Hood Granny, and I've brought you some cakes and eggs and cream, and a little pot of butter."

"Lift up the latch and come in."

So Red Riding Hood lifted the latch and went in and walked towards the bed. "Come closer Little Red Riding Hood and sit beside me."

Little Red Riding Hood opened her eyes wide when she saw the strange-looking Grandmother. "Oh, Grandmother what great arms you have!"

"All the better to hug you with my dear."

"Grandmother, what great ears you have!"

"All the better to hear you with my dear."

"Grandmother, what great eyes you have!"

"All the better to see you with my dear."

"Oh, Grandmother what great big teeth you have!"

"All the better to eat you up my dear."

And as he said that, the wicked wolf jumped up

in bed to spring on Little Red Riding Hood and gobble her up. His legs got tied up for a minute in the sheets, and Little Red Riding Hood dropped her basket and ran to the door calling for help. She just got to the door when the wolf sprang off the bed, and reached the door too ready to gobble her up. Just at that moment, Red Riding Hood's father, who knew she was taking a basket of food to her Grandmother, thought he would see how Granny was too, and to take Red Riding Hood home for lunch. He was horrified to see the wolf still with Granny's spectacles and her nightcap on, just about to jump on top of Little Red Riding Hood and gobble her up. The father leapt forward and struck the wicked wolf one fierce blow with his woodman's axe. And that was the end of that wicked wolf. "Oh father, I'm so glad to see you. I'll do as mummy says, and never talk to anyone I don't know ever again."

"Little Red Riding Hood, where is your Grandmother?"

"I don't know father. I thought she was in bed there, but it was the wicked wolf instead. Oh, I was so frightened."

"We must find her at once. The wolf can't have, oh surely, he can't have eaten your Grandmother. What's that?"

"I think the sound came from over in that corner. Oh, hold my hand father I'm frightened it might be another wolf."

"No, someone's locked up in the cupboard. Wait, Grandmother, are you alright? Here, let me untie that scarf across your mouth and help you out. Oh my dears, oh it was dreadful! It was dreadful and, but but you came in time. Just help me back to bed. I'll be alright thank-you, thank-you."

"There you are Grandmother, and here's the basket of cakes and eggs and cream, and a little pot of butter. Now father, can we go back home to mother please?"

THE THREE LITTLE PIGS

Once upon a time there were three little pigs, and they decided they to build themselves a house each. The first little pig built himself a neat little house of straw. The second little pig built his house of sticks. But the third little pig built his house of bricks. By and by, along came Mr. Wolf to the first little pig's house.

"Little pig, little pig let me in."

But the little pig knew the bad wolf's voice and he called out, "No, no not by the hair of my chinny chin chin, I will not, will not let you in."

"Then I'll huff and I'll puff and I'll blow your house in."

So he huffed and he puffed till he blew the house in. But the first little pig just had time while the wolf was getting his breath back, to rush as hard as he could to the second pig's little house made of sticks. "Oh, I just got here, close the door quick!"

And they lived happily together for a while. But by

and by, Mr. Wolf passed the house made of sticks and he thought to himself, "I smell pig. Little pig, little pig let me in."

But the second little pig peeped through a crack in the door, and he called, "no, nobody here of my chinny, chin chin, I will not let you in."

"Then I'll huff and I'll puff and I'll blow your house in."

So the wolf huffed and he puffed and huffed, until he blew the house of sticks right in. But the two little pigs didn't wait till the wolf got his breath back. They ran and they ran until they reached the third little pig's house made of brick.

"Oh, we just made it, close the door quick!"

Of course, it had taken a lot longer to build, but it was stronger and the three little pigs felt safe and happy. But pretty soon Mr. Wolf came sniffing around, and he crept up to the door and smelt the little pigs inside. "Little pig, little pig let me in."

"No, no by the hair of my chinny chin chin, I will not let you in."

"Then I'll huff and I'll puff and blow your house in."

And he huffed and he puffed, and he puffed and he huffed, but he couldn't blow that house in. Then the wolf sat down to think, and he knocked at the house again.

"Little pig, little pig I can tell you where there are some nice turnips."

"Where are the turnips?"

"In the field at the top of the lane. I'll meet you at six o'clock tomorrow morning and we'll go there together."

"Yes, I'll be ready."

But the third little pig got up at five o'clock and ran down the lane, and was safely home with the turnips when the wolf knocked at six o'clock. "Little pig, are you ready?"

"Ready, I've been and come back with the turnips."

The wolf was very cross but said, "little pig, I know a tree where there are some beautiful apples."

"Oh, where are those apples?"

"At a tree in a field in the next lane. Be sure you are ready at five o'clock."

But next morning the little pig got up at four o'clock, climbed the tree and picked the apples. But Mr. Wolf had got up early too, and there he was standing under the tree waiting. "Why didn't you wait for me little pig? Are they nice apples?"

"Very nice, let me throw you one."

But he threw the apple as far as he could, and while the wolf ran to get it, the little pig jumped down and ran as fast as he could to his little house, and slammed the door just in time.

Next day, Mr. Wolf knocked and called out, "little, pig, little pig there is a fair in the village today. Will you come to it with me? Be ready at three o'clock."

"Oh yes, I'll be ready."

But the little pig went very early to the fair, bought a wooden barrel for a butter churn, and when he was nearly home he saw the wolf. Oh, he was very frightened and jumped inside the butter churn. It tipped on its side and went rolling down the hill. This frightened Mr. Wolf and he ran into the woods. But next day he was back at the little brick house. "Little pig, little pig let me in."

"Oh, no, no, no by the hair of my chinny, chin chin."

"Then I'll huff and I'll puff and I'll blow your house in."

Then the wolf began quietly to climb up onto the roof. Very quietly the three little pigs built up the fire, and soon a big pot of water was really boiling. They heard the wolf coming down the chimney after them.

"Come on wolf, come on, come on."

And the wolf got so cross and so excited that he came down far too quickly, and fell 'plop' into the pan of boiling water.

"Aaargh," and that was the end of the wicked wolf! And the three little pigs stayed together safely and happily in their dear little brick house.